WITHDRAWN

PowerKids Readers:

The Bilingual Library of the
United States of America™

*Bilingual Edition
English/Spanish
Edición bilingüe*

NEW JERSEY
NUEVA JERSEY

VANESSA BROWN

TRADUCCIÓN AL ESPAÑOL: MARÍA CRISTINA BRUSCA

The Rosen Publishing Group's
PowerKids Press™ & **Editorial Buenas Letras**™
New York

Published in 2006 by The Rosen Publishing Group, Inc.
29 East 21st Street, New York, NY 10010

First Edition

Photo Credits: Cover © Bob Krist/Corbis; p. 5 © Joseph Sohm; Visions of America/Corbis; p. 7 © 2002 Geoatlas; pp. 9, 31 (cliff) © Tony Linck/Corbis; p. 11 © North Wind Picture Archives; pp. 13, 15, 17, 31 (Barton, Cleveland, Sinatra, light bulb) © Bettmann/Corbis; p. 19 © Joe McDonald/Corbis; p. 21 © Wally McNamee/Corbis; p. 23 © Robert Essel NYC/Corbis; pp. 25, 30 (capital) © Alan Goldsmith/Corbis; pp. 26, 30 (red oak) © G. Kalt/Corbis; p. 30 (purple violet) © Buddy Mays/Corbis; p. 30 (eastern gold-finch) © James L. Amos/Corbis; p. 30 (Garden State) © Kelly-Mooney Photography/Corbis; p. 30 (brook trout) © Dale C. Spartas/Corbis; p. 31 (Lange) © Ansel Adams Publishing Rights Trust/Corbis; p. 31 (Ginsberg) © William Coupon/Corbis; p. 31 (Springsteen) © Neal Preston/Corbis; p. 31 (medicine) © Ed Bock/Corbis.

Library of Congress Cataloging-in-Publication Data

Brown, Vanessa, 1963–
New Jersey = Nueva Jersey / Vanessa Brown ; traducción al español, María Cristina Brusca. —1st ed.
p. cm. – (The bilingual library of the United States of America) Includes bibliographical references and index.
ISBN 1-4042-3095-5 (library binding)
1. New Jersey—Juvenile literature. I. Title: Nueva Jersey. II. Title. III. Series.
F134.3.B765 2006
974.9—dc22
                                                     2005016972

Manufactured in the United States of America

Due to the changing nature of Internet links, Editorial Buenas Letras has developed an online list of Web sites related to the subject of this book. This site is updated regularly. Please use this link to access the list:

http://www.buenasletraslinks.com/ls/newjersey

Contents

1 Welcome to New Jersey   4

2 New Jersey Geography   6

3 New Jersey History   10

4 Living in New Jersey   18

5 New Jersey Today   22

6 Let's Draw New Jersey's State Tree   26

Timeline/New Jersey Events   28–29

New Jersey Facts   30

Famous New Jerseyites/Words to Know   31

Resources/Word Count/Index   32

Contenido

1 Bienvenidos a Nueva Jersey   4

2 Geografía de Nueva Jersey   6

3 Historia de Nueva Jersey   10

4 La vida en Nueva Jersey   18

5 Nueva Jersey, hoy   22

6 Dibujemos el árbol del estado de Nueva Jersey   26

Cronología/ Eventos en Nueva Jersey   28–29

Datos sobre Nueva Jersey   30

Neojerseítas famosos/ Palabras que debes saber   31

Recursos/ Número de palabras/ Índice   32

Welcome to New Jersey

These are the flag and seal of the state of New Jersey. The seal has a banner with the state motto. It says "Liberty and Prosperity."

Bienvenidos a Nueva Jersey

Estos son la bandera y el escudo de Nueva Jersey. El escudo tiene una banda con el lema del estado. El lema dice "Libertad y prosperidad".

4

New Jersey Flag and State Seal

Bandera y escudo del estado de Nueva Jersey

New Jersey Geography

New Jersey borders the states of Delaware, Pennsylvania, and New York. The Hudson River, the Atlantic Ocean, the Delaware Bay, and the Delaware River also border New Jersey.

Geografía de Nueva Jersey

Nueva Jersey linda con los estados de Delaware, Pensilvania y Nueva York. El río Hudson, el océano Atlántico, la bahía Delaware y el río Delaware también limitan con Nueva Jersey.

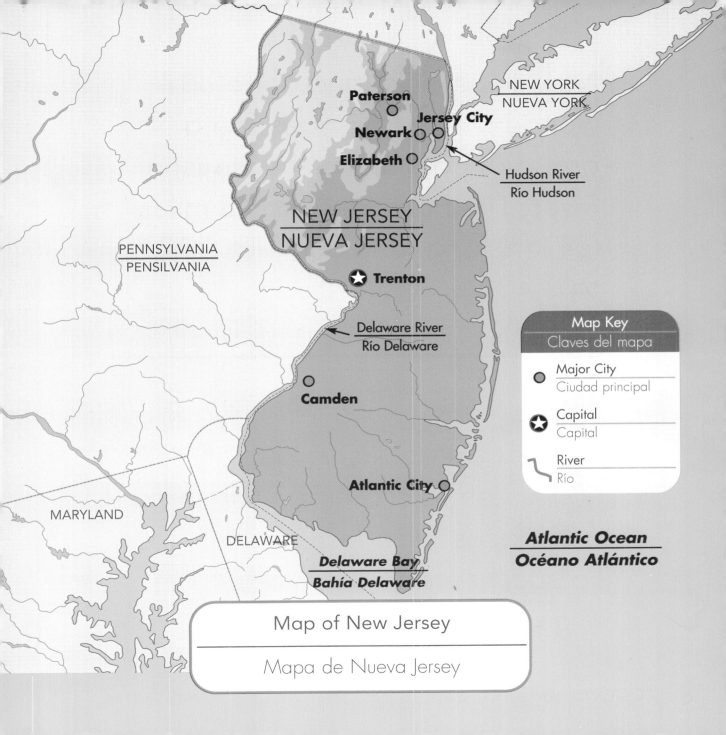

NEW YORK
NUEVA YORK

Paterson

Jersey City

Newark

Elizabeth

Hudson River
Río Hudson

NEW JERSEY
NUEVA JERSEY

PENNSYLVANIA
PENSILVANIA

Trenton

Delaware River
Río Delaware

Camden

MARYLAND

Atlantic City

DELAWARE

Delaware Bay
Bahía Delaware

Map Key
Claves del mapa

Major City
Ciudad principal

Capital
Capital

River
Río

Atlantic Ocean
Océano Atlántico

Map of New Jersey

Mapa de Nueva Jersey

New Jersey is a land of natural wonders. The Palisades are a group of cliffs along the Hudson River. The Palisades are 15 miles (24 km) long and 500 feet (152 m) tall.

Nueva Jersey es una tierra de maravillas naturales. A lo largo del río Hudson se encuentra un grupo de acantilados llamados Palisades. Los Palisades tienen 15 millas (24 km) de largo y 500 pies (152 m) de altura.

Palisades, New Jersey

Palisades, Nueva Jersey

New Jersey History

Dutch explorers reached New Jersey in 1614. The Dutch claimed the land and named it New Netherlands. In 1664, the British took control and New Jersey became a British colony.

Historia de Nueva Jersey

Los exploradores holandeses llegaron a Nueva Jersey en 1614. Los holandeses reclamaron la tierra y la llamaron Nueva Holanda. En 1664, los británicos tomaron el control y Nueva Jersey pasó a ser una colonia británica.

Philip Carteret, New Jersey's First English Governor

Philip Carteret, primer gobernador inglés de Nueva Jersey

In 1775, the colonies went to war against the British. New Jersey played an important part in this war. This war is known as the American Revolution (1775–1783). The Battle of Trenton was an important victory for the colonies.

En 1775, las colonias comenzaron una guerra contra los británicos. Nueva Jersey tuvo un papel muy importante en esta guerra. Esta guerra formó parte de la Guerra de Independencia (1775–1783). La batalla de Trenton fue una importante victoria para las colonias.

George Washington and Revolutionary Troops
Crossing the Delaware River

George Washington y las tropas revolucionarias,
cruzan el río Delaware

Mary Hays McCaul, known as Molly Pitcher, was a heroine of the American Revolution. Molly brought pitchers of water to the thirsty troops during the Battle of Monmouth.

Mary Hays McCaul, conocida como Molly Pitcher, es una heroína de la Guerra de Independencia. Molly les llevó jarras (*pitchers*) de agua a las tropas sedientas durante la Batalla de Monmouth.

Molly Pitcher was born in Trenton, New Jersey, in 1754

Molly Pitcher nació en Trenton, Nueva Jersey, en 1754

Thomas Alva Edison was a scientist and an inventor. In 1876, he opened a laboratory in Menlo Park, New Jersey. Edison invented the electric lightbulb there.

Thomas Alva Edison fue un científico e inventor. En 1876, estableció su laboratorio en Menlo Park, Nueva Jersey. En este lugar, Edison inventó la bombilla eléctrica.

Thomas Edison in His Laboratory

Thomas Edison en su laboratorio

Living in New Jersey

New Jersey is known as the Garden State. The state has more than 10,000 farms that produce fruits and vegetables, like blueberries, cranberries, peaches, lettuce, corn, tomatoes, and bell peppers.

La vida en Nueva Jersey

Nueva Jersey se conoce como el Estado Jardín. Este estado tiene más de 10,000 granjas que producen frutas y verduras como arándanos, duraznos, lechuga, maíz, tomates y pimientos.

Cranberry Harvest in Chatsworth, New Jersey

Cosecha de arándanos en Chatsworth, Nueva Jersey

Although New Jersey is the fifth-smallest state in the United States, it has the ninth-largest number of people. People from all over the world live in New Jersey today.

Nueva Jersey es el quinto estado más pequeño de los Estados Unidos. Pero, pese a su tamaño, es el noveno estado más poblado del país. Hoy en día, gente de todo el mundo vive en Nueva Jersey.

New Jerseyites During a Public Meeting

Neojerseítas durante una reunión pública

New Jersey Today

New Jersey factories are very important for the state. New Jersey is a leader in the production of chemical products, like cleaners. New Jersey also makes medicines and food products.

Nueva Jersey, hoy

Las fábricas de Nueva Jersey son muy importantes para el estado. Nueva Jersey es líder en la fabricación de productos químicos, como jabón. Nueva Jersey también produce medicamentos y productos alimenticios.

Medicine Production

Producción de medicamentos

Newark, Jersey City, Paterson, and Elizabeth are important cities in New Jersey. Trenton is the capital of the state.

Newark, Jersey City, Paterson y Elizabeth son ciudades importantes de Nueva Jersey. Trenton es la capital del estado.

New Jersey State House

Casa de gobierno de Nueva Jersey

Activity:
Let's Draw New Jersey's State Tree

The red oak became New Jersey's state tree in 1950.

Actividad:
Dibujemos el árbol del estado de Nueva Jersey

El roble rojo es el árbol del estado de Nueva Jersey desde 1950.

1

Draw the trunk and the branches with wavy lines. There are five main branches in this tree.

Dibuja el tronco y las ramas con líneas onduladas. En este árbol hay cinco ramas principales.

2

Turn your pencil on its side, and lightly shade the area on top of the trunk with short up-and-down strokes.

Poniendo el lápiz de costado sombrea ligeramente el área de la copa, con trazos cortos y de arriba hacia abajo.

3

Continue to shade the tree. Press harder on your pencil. These are the leaves.

Continúa sombreando el árbol, presionando con más fuerza el lápiz, para representar las hojas.

4

Now shade the trunk, and you are done!

Ahora sombrea el tronco, ¡y habrás acabado!

Timeline

Cronología

Giovanni da Verrazano explores the New Jersey coast.	**1524**	Giovanni da Verrazano explora la costa de Nueva Jersey.
Bergen, now Jersey City, becomes the first permanent town in New Jersey.	**1660**	Bergen, la actual Jersey City, es el primer poblado permanente de Nueva Jersey.
The British take control of New Jersey from the Dutch.	**1664**	Los británicos asumen el control de Nueva Jersey, desplazando a los holandeses.
Princeton and Trenton serve as the nation's capital.	**1783–1784**	Princeton y Trenton sirven como capital de la nación.
The first amusement pier over the ocean is built in Atlantic City.	**1882**	Se construye el primer parque de diversiones sobre un muelle, en Atlantic City.
New Jersey governor Woodrow Wilson is elected president of the United States.	**1912**	El gobernador de Nueva Jersey, Woodrow Wilson, es elegido presidente de los Estados Unidos.
The Holland Tunnel opens.	**1927**	Se abre el Túnel Holland.
The New Jersey Devils win the Stanley Cup.	**1995**	Los New Jersey Devils ganan la copa Stanley.
The USS *New Jersey* battleship becomes a museum.	**2001**	El barco de guerra U.S.S. New Jersey se transforma en un museo.

New Jersey Events

March
Washington's Birthday Celebration in Titusville

April
Cherry Blossom Display in Newark
New Jersey Folk Festival in New Brunswick

June
New Jersey's Seafood Festival in Belmar
National Marbles Tournament in Wildwood

July
Withesbog Blueberry Festival in Browns Mills
New Jersey Festival of Ballooning in Readington

August
Sussex County Farm and Horse Show

October
Cranberry Festival in Chatsworth

December
Victorian Christmas Celebration in Cape May

Eventos en Nueva Jersey

Marzo
Celebración del cumpleaños de Washington, en Titusville

Abril
Muestra de la flor del cerezo, en Newark
Festival folclórico de Nueva Jersey, en New Brunswick

Junio
Festival de los pescados y mariscos de Nueva Jersey, en Belmar
Torneo nacional de canicas, en Wildwood

Julio
Festival Withesbog del arándano, en Brown Mills
Festival Nueva Jersey de globos, en Readington

Agosto
Exposición rural y torneo hípico del condado de Sussex

Octubre
Festival del arándano, en Chatsworth

Diciembre
Celebración de la Navidad victoriana, en Cape May

New Jersey Facts/Datos sobre Nueva Jersey

Population
8.4 million

Población
8.4 millones

Capital
Trenton

Capital
Trenton

State Motto
Liberty and
Prosperity

Lema del estado
Libertad y prosperidad

State Flower
Purple violet

Flor del estado
Violeta púrpura

State Bird
Eastern goldfinch

Ave del estado
Pinzón oriental

State Nickname
Garden State

Mote del estado
El Estado Jardín

State Tree
Red Oak

Árbol del estado
Roble rojo

State Fish
Brook Trout

Pez del estado
Trucha silvestre

Famous Newjerseyites/Neojerseítas famosos

Clara Barton
(1821–1912)

American Red Cross founder
Fundadora de la Cruz Roja Americana

Grover Cleveland
(1837–1908)

U.S. president
Presidente de E.U.A.

Dorothea Lange
(1895–1965)

Photographer
Fotógrafa

Frank Sinatra
(1915–1998)

Singer
Cantante

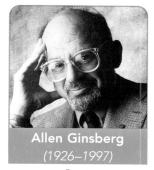

Allen Ginsberg
(1926–1997)

Poet
Poeta

Bruce Springsteen
(1949–   )

Musician
Músico

Words to Know/Palabras que debes saber

border
frontera

cliff
acantilado

lightbulb
bombilla
eléctrica

medicines
medicamentos

Here are more books to read about New Jersey:
Otros libros que puedes leer sobre Nueva Jersey:

In English/En inglés:
New Jersey
Rookie Read-About Geography
by Evento, Susan
Children's Press, 2005

In Spanish/En español:
Nueva Jersey: El Estado Jardín
World Almanac
by Siegfried Holtz, Eric, Porras
Carlos, D'Andrea Patricia
(Translators)
World Almanac Library, 2003

Words in English: 319

Palabras en español: 326

Index

A
American Revolution, 12

B
borders, 6

E
Edison, Thomas Alva, 16

F
flag, 4

H
Hudson River, 6, 8

N
New Netherlands, 10

P
Palisades, the, 8
Pitcher, Molly, 14

S
seal, 4

Índice

B
bandera, 4

E
Edison, Thomas Alva, 16
escudo, 4

F
fronteras, 6

G
Guerra de Independencia, 12

N
Nueva Holanda, 10

P
Palisades, 8
Pitcher, Molly, 14

R
Río Hudson, 6, 8